Fish Had a Wish

Michael Garland

Holiday House / New York

Copyright © 2012 by Michael Garland
All Rights Reserved
HOLIDAY HOUSE is registered in the U.S. Patent and Trademark Office.
Printed and Bound in November 2011 at Tien Wah Press, Johor Bahru, Johor, Malaysia.
The text typeface is Report School.
The artwork was created in digi-wood.
www.holidayhouse.com
First Edition
1 3 5 7 9 10 8 6 4 2

Library of Congress Cataloging-in-Publication Data
Garland, Michael, 1952-
Fish had a wish / by Michael Garland. — 1st ed.
p. cm. — (I like to read)
Summary: Fish wishes to be all sorts of animals because each one is special,
then realizes there is something good about being a fish, too.
ISBN 978-0-8234-2394-1 (hardcover)
[1. Wishes—Fiction. 2. Contentment—Fiction. 3. Self-acceptance—Fiction.
4. Fishes—Fiction. 5. Animals—Fiction.] I. Title.
PZ7.G18413Fis 2012
[E]—dc22
2010050124

To my mother

Fish had a wish.

"I wish I were a bird!"
said Fish.
"I could fly high up
in the sky."

"I wish I were a turtle.
I could take a nap
on a sunny rock."

"I wish I were a skunk.
I could make a big stink!"

"If I were a bobcat,
I could have spots."

"If I were a bee,
I could buzz
from flower to flower."

"I could be a beaver
and build a big dam."

"I could be a butterfly
with pretty wings."

"I wish I were a snake.
HISSSSSSSS."

A mayfly landed on the water.
Fish ate the bug with one bite.
"That was *so* good!"
said Fish.

"It is good to be a fish.
I wish to *stay* a fish.
Yes!
To stay a fish is
what I wish."